Doctor Ted

by Andrea Beaty and Pascal Lemaitre

MARGARET K. McELDERRY BOOKS

NEW YORK   LONDON   TORONTO   SYDNEY

For Michael, my love

—A. B.

To Doctor Claude Haber

—P. L.

Margaret K. McElderry Books
An imprint of Simon & Schuster
Children's Publishing Division
1230 Avenue of the Americas
New York, New York 10020
Text copyright © 2008 by Andrea Beaty
Illustrations copyright © 2008 by
Pascal Lemaitre
All rights reserved, including the right of
reproduction in whole or in part in any form.
Book design by Ann Bobco
The text for this book is set in Bliss.
The illustrations for this book are rendered
in brush and ink, then colored digitally.
Manufactured in China
1 2 3 4 5 6 7 8 9 10
Library of Congress Cataloging-in-
Publication Data
Beaty, Andrea.
Doctor Ted / by Andrea Beaty ; illustrated by
Pascal Lemaitre. —1st. ed.
p. cm.
Summary: After bumping his knee one
morning, Ted decides to become a doctor,
but he has only one problem—
he has no patients!
ISBN 978-1-4424-5423-1
[1. Physicians—Fiction. 2. Medical care—
Fiction. 3. Imagination—Fiction.]
I. Lemaitre, Pascal, ill. II. Title.
PZ7.B380547Do 2008
[E]—dc22 2006003191
1211 SCP

One morning
Ted woke up,
got out of bed, and
bumped his knee.

That's not good, thought Ted.
I need a doctor.

He looked everywhere,

but he couldn't find one.

And since Ted couldn't find a doctor . . .

... he became a doctor.

Doctor Ted didn't have an office,
so he made one.

Doctor Ted didn't have a big bandage,
so he made one of those too.

Now all I need is a patient,
he thought.

He sat and waited for one to arrive.

He waited . . .

and he waited . . .

and he waited.

Nice waiting room, thought Doctor Ted.

Then he waited some more.

I think it's time for a house call, he thought.

"Hello?" he called throughout the house.

His mother was in the kitchen.

"You have measles,"
said Doctor Ted.
"We should operate."

"Those are my freckles,"
said his mother.
"Eat your breakfast."

At school Doctor Ted sat in
the third row of Mrs. Johnson's class.
All around him, students coughed
and sniffled and sneezed.

Doctor Ted smiled.

　　Patients, he thought.

The patients were very germy.

At lunch Doctor Ted took their temperatures and measured their blood pressure.

He gave them fine medical advice, and they were very thankful.

Doctor Ted was such a good doctor, even Mrs. Johnson came to see him.

"You can't practice medicine in the lunchroom!" she said.

"You have mumps," said Doctor Ted. "Crutches could help."

"Those are my cheeks," said Mrs. Johnson. "Eat your lunch."

Principal Bigham walked in.

Doctor Ted could tell
he was very sick.
He needed a doctor.

"We already have a school doctor
who visits on Fridays," Principal Bigham
said with a smile.

"You have gingivitis," said Doctor Ted. "You need a full-body cast."

Principal Bigham frowned.

"You also have
bad breath,"
said Doctor Ted.
"You need a shot."

The principal's face turned bright red.

"And a fever!" said Doctor Ted.
"You need a transplant."

"WE ALREADY HAVE A SCHOOL DOCTOR!"

Principal Bigham
pointed toward the door.

"We could do something about that foot odor," said Doctor Ted.

"Go home!" said Principal Bigham.

Doctor Ted was very sad. He packed up his big bandage and went home.

That night he took two cookies and went straight to bed.

The next day during recess,
Ted sat on a bench and sighed.

He watched Frances Sylvester do
gymnastics on the monkey bars.
She was very talented.

Everyone thought so, especially Mrs. Johnson and Principal Bigham.

Frances finished her routine
with a triple twisting-
somersault.

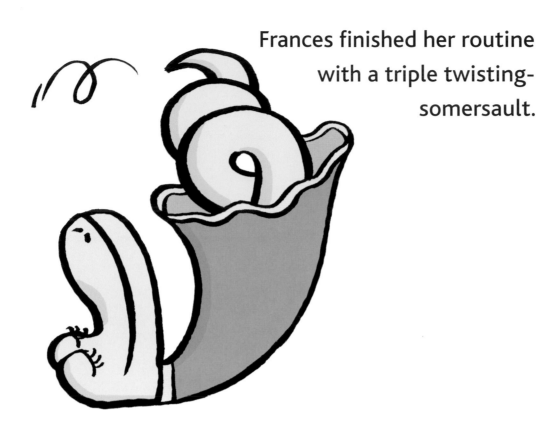

She landed on Mrs. Johnson.

"OUCH!"
cried Mrs. Johnson.
"My ankle!"

Principal Bigham ran this way and that.

"HELP!" he yelled.
"Call an ambulance!
Call the fire department!
Call the library!
JUST CALL SOMEBODY!"

But Doctor Ted was already there.

He wrapped Mrs. Johnson's ankle with his big bandage. He checked her vision and her tonsils.

"Take two cookies," he said.
"You'll feel better in the morning."

Just then, the ambulance arrived.
And the fire department.
And the librarians.

"It's a good thing you had Doctor Ted," they all said.
"There's always room for another school doctor," said Mrs. Johnson.
"My work here is done," said Doctor Ted. "Keep the bandage."

Principal Bigham's face turned bright red. "You *really* should do something about that fever," said Doctor Ted.

That night Doctor Ted closed his office, packed away his stethoscope, . . .

and went to sleep,
knowing he had done
a good job.

The next morning Ted woke up, got out of bed, and sniffed the air. It smelled like burnt toast.

That's not good, thought Ted.
I need a fire truck. . . .